Ancient Forest

To Desert

Bird Meeting Place

Cockatoo Nesting Trees

Emu Running Track

Underground Caves

Snake Gully

Kangaroo Grass Plains

Toad Island

Platypus River Bank

Marshlands

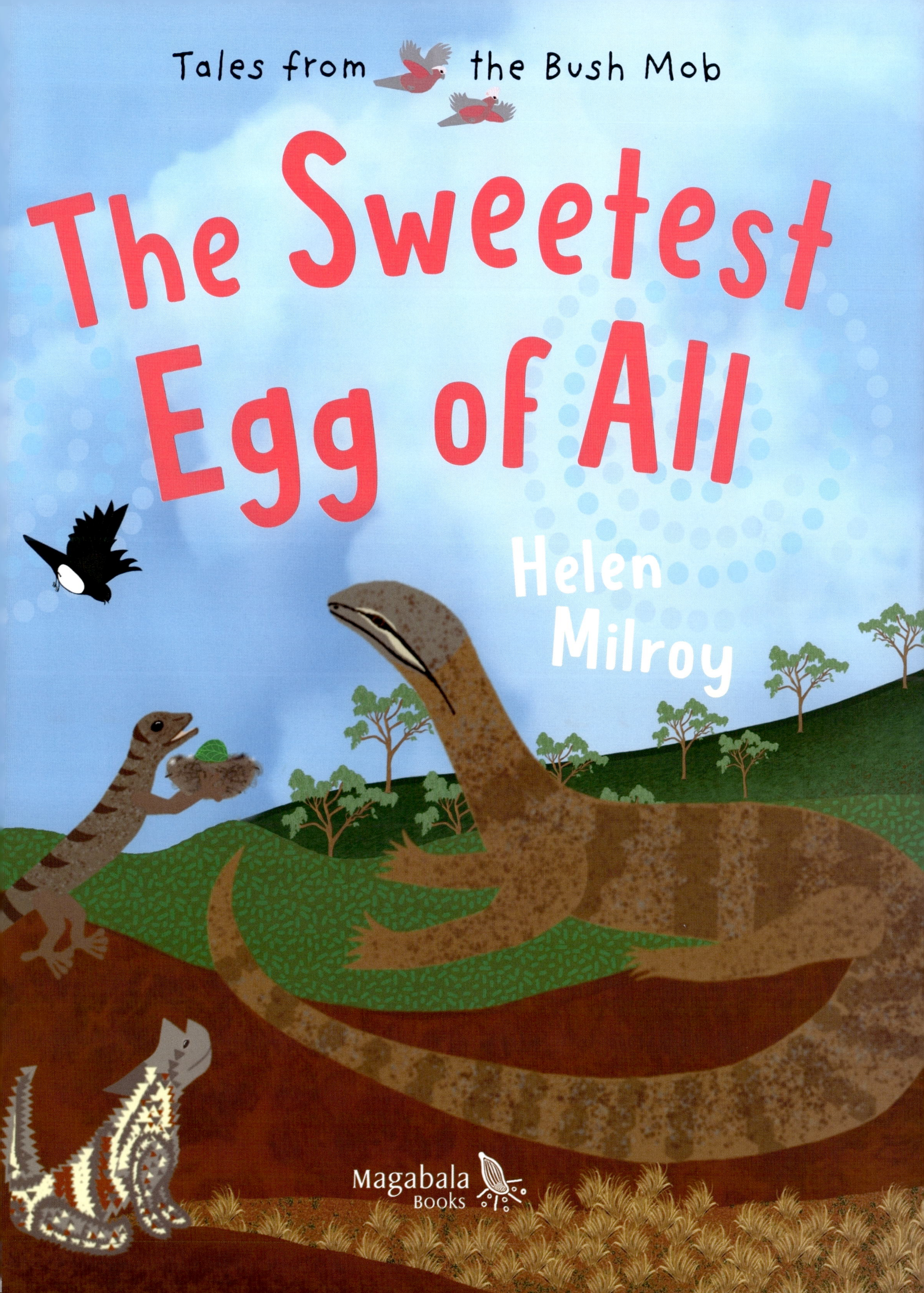
Tales from the Bush Mob
The Sweetest Egg of All
Helen Milroy
Magabala Books

LEADING PUBLISHER OF ABORIGINAL AND
TORRES STRAIT ISLANDER STORYTELLERS.

CHANGING THE WORLD, ONE STORY AT A TIME.

First published 2022,
Magabala Books Aboriginal Corporation, Broome, Western Australia
Website: www.magabala.com
Email: sales@magabala.com

Magabala Books receives financial assistance from the Commonwealth Government through the Australia Council, its arts advisory body. The State of Western Australia has made an investment in this project through the Department of Local Government, Sport and Cultural Industries. Magabala Books would like to acknowledge the generous support of the Shire of Broome, Western Australia.

Magabala Books is Australia's only independent Aboriginal and Torres Strait Islander publishing house. Magabala Books acknowledges the Traditional Owners of the Country on which we live and work. We recognise the unbroken connection to traditional lands, waters and cultures. Through what we publish, we honour all our Elders, peoples and stories, past, present and future.

The illustrations for this book were created digitally.
Design concept John Canty
Cover design Jo Hunt

Printed in China by Everbest Printing Company

ISBN Print 978-1-922613-08-0
ISBN ePDF 978-1-922613-09-7

A catalogue record for this book is available from the National Library of Australia

Department of Local Government, Sport and Cultural Industries
lotterywest

About the series

Welcome to the third book in the Tales from the Bush Mob series.

The Bush Mob is a group of birds and animals who live together in outback Australia. They go on lots of adventures, solve many problems and learn how to look after each other. They meet other animals who come to visit or who need their help and they always come up with a solution!

In this third book in the series you will meet Gecko, Thorny Devil and Scrubby Python who want to give Bungarra the best birthday present. They hear from King George Brown (KGB) that Willy Wagtail's egg is the sweetest egg of all and hatch a cunning plan to steal one for Bungarra. But KGB has different plans and Dingo and the Bush Mob must go into action to save the day.

Here are some of the birds and animals you will meet in this book:

Gecko

Bungarra

Thorny Devil

Scrubby Python

King Toad

Echidna

King George Brown (KGB)

Kookaburra

Platypus

Koala

Willy Wagtail

Wombat

Dingo

Kangaroo

Emu

Bungarra's Birthday Surprise

Bungarra loved nothing better than to get up early and take his morning stroll along the riverbank. He loved watching the sun wake up and spread its light across the landscape.

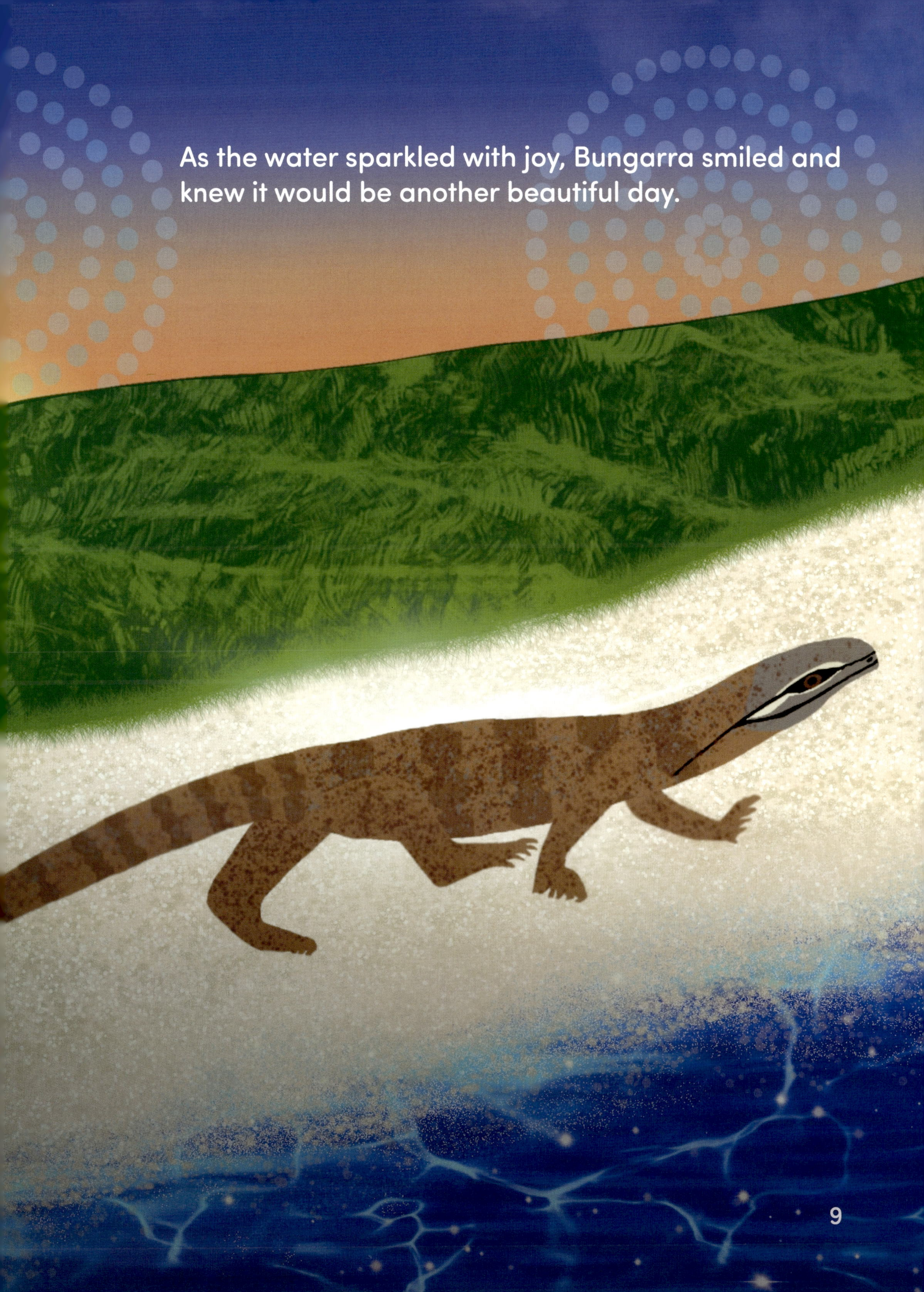

As the water sparkled with joy, Bungarra smiled and knew it would be another beautiful day.

Gecko would always scamper along behind with Thorny Devil. They both loved Bungarra and really wanted to be a big lizard just like him. They tried to be like Bungarra by walking with their tails straight but they just couldn't manage it, especially Thorny Devil.

Each time he tried, his prickly, curvy tail would spring back into place.

Bungarra was especially happy this morning as it was the beginning of his birthday week. Gecko and Thorny Devil would bring Bungarra a treat every day and, at the end of the week, Gecko promised Bungarra would receive the best birthday present ever.

Of course, Gecko had no idea what he was going to get Bungarra and was asking everyone else for suggestions.

King George Brown (KGB) heard about this and told Gecko he knew exactly what Bungarra would like. KGB had heard a long time ago that Willy Wagtail's egg was the sweetest egg of all. KGB had a real sweet tooth, and he was wily – he had changed his name as he thought King Brown was way too plain. He had heard of a famous King called George from far away so he added George to his name to make himself sound royal and important.

He had always wanted to steal one of the eggs but could not get up into the tree. KGB told Gecko that the best present of all would be a Willy Wagtail's egg and that he would help him to get it.

Of course what KGB didn't know was that Willy Wagtail's egg did not taste sweet at all. It was called 'sweet' because it was so small and cute.

The Plan and the Plot

Gecko wasn't sure what to do, so he went to speak with Thorny Devil to come up with a plan.

They thought of a way to get the egg but needed the help of Scrubby Python. Scrubby Python was the longest snake in the bush community. He was so long he often slithered over his own tail and sometimes accidentally tied himself in knots. Gecko often helped Scrubby Python out of his troubles, so they had been good friends for quite a while.

Gecko, Thorny Devil and Scrubby Python met up in the special meeting place to work out what to do.

Over the next few days Gecko and
Thorny Devil started collecting
small twigs and twine as well as
looking for fur and feathers.

They built a small nest that could be stuck onto the spikes on Thorny Devil's back and lined it with the fur and feathers.

When the fake nest was ready, they told KGB.

Now, KGB had persuaded the birds that he needed to teach them a special birthday song for Bungarra, and he planned a practice session to get the birds out of the way.

While the birds were away, Gecko, Thorny Devil and Scrubby Python arrived at Willy Wagtail's tree. Gecko and Scrubby Python climbed up the tree while Thorny Devil waited below with the fake nest on his back.

Gecko very carefully picked up the precious egg from Willy Wagtail's nest and rolled it all the way down from the tree on Scrubby Python's belly. It tickled so much that Scrubby Python started laughing and almost lost the egg. Thankfully it landed safely in the fake nest!

Gecko, Thorny Devil and Scrubby Python placed the nest in a cave, which KGB had assured them would be safe until Bungarra's birthday.

But Gecko, Thorny Devil and Scrubby Python didn't know that KGB had been secretly meeting with the king of the cane toads. King Toad had agreed to take the nest from the cave and hide it on Toad Island in the middle of the marshlands until KGB could collect it. King Toad and KGB had known each other for a long time. Most of the community were scared of KGB and the cane toads because they were so grumpy and had such poisonous venom.

King Toad and KGB both thought they should be boss of the whole community as they were both kings. But that was never going to happen while Boss Dog Dingo was head of the Bush Mob Council. Anyway, the cane toad wasn't a real king, he just called himself 'King' because he was the largest toad.

When Willy Wagtail finished choir practice, she went back to her nest only to discover her egg was missing!

She went straight to Dingo who called an emergency meeting of the Council.

Koala told the Council that when she was sitting in her tree, she had seen Gecko and Thorny Devil making a nest from twigs and twine. She had asked them what they were doing but they just giggled and scampered off. It seemed strange at the time but now it made sense.

Dingo decided to look for Gecko and find out what was going on. He heard a commotion at a nearby cave and went to see what was happening.

Bungarra, Gecko and Thorny Devil were inside having an argument. Dingo asked them what was going on. Gecko confessed that he had stolen Willy Wagtail's egg for Bungarra's birthday. But when he took Bungarra to the cave for his birthday surprise, the nest and the egg were gone. Gecko told Dingo that KGB had helped plan the birthday surprise but that he didn't show up when he said he would. Dingo knew KGB and he became very, very suspicious.

They looked around the cave for clues and noticed some muddy toad footprints.

Dingo went to find KGB, but he was nowhere to be seen.

Dingo went back to the Council for help.

Platypus said KGB and King Toad were best friends. Dingo asked Platypus to see what the toads were up to. The cane toads had come from another country and had taken over the marshlands. King Toad lived on Toad Island in the middle of the swamp. The marshlands were dark and scary and no-one ever went there, but Platypus was brave.

Platypus could see a small egg hidden under a tree stump on Toad Island. He quickly swam away before he was seen by the toads that were guarding it and returned to the Council to tell the others. They were convinced this was Willy Wagtail's egg.

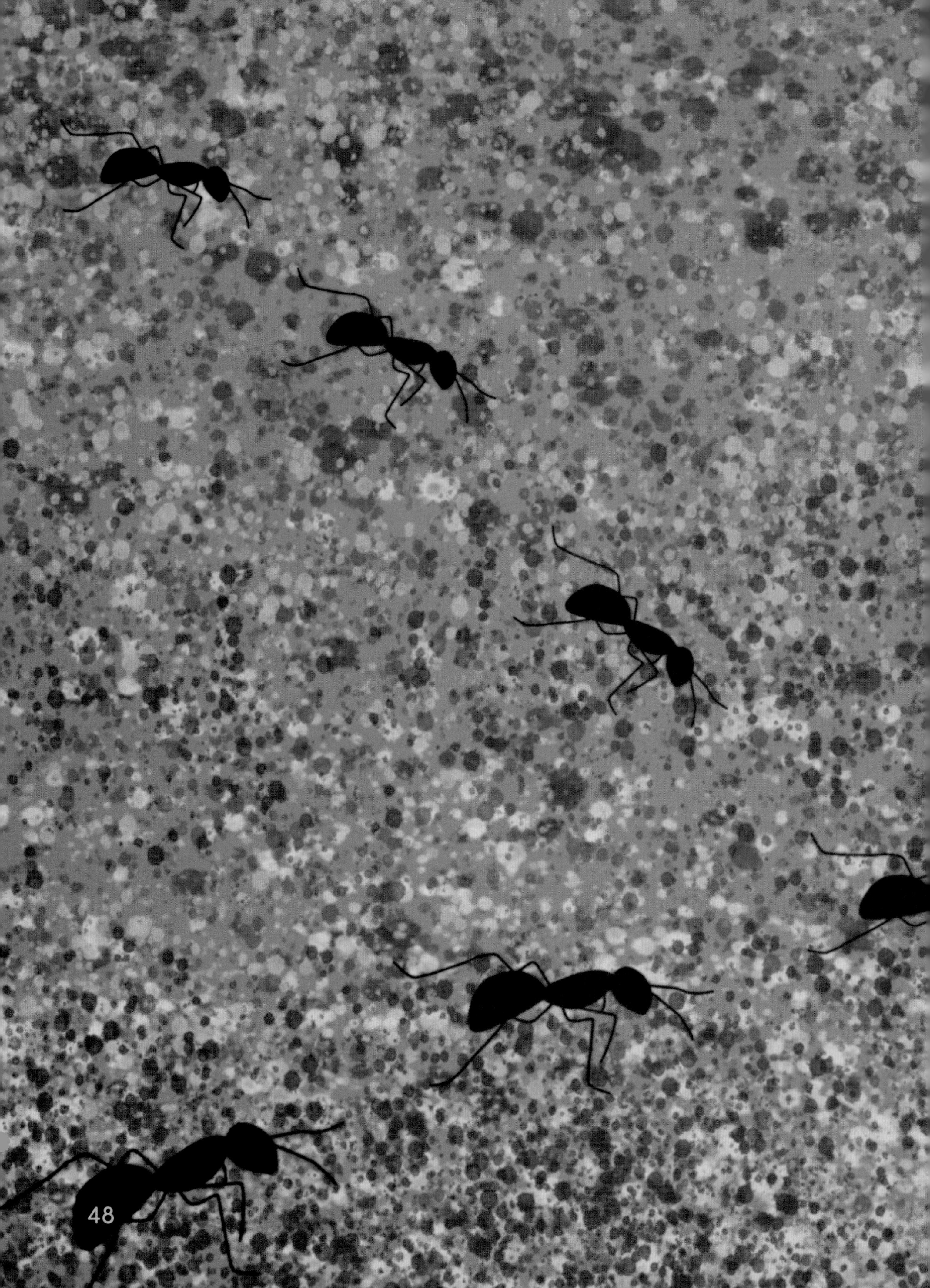

The Big Rescue

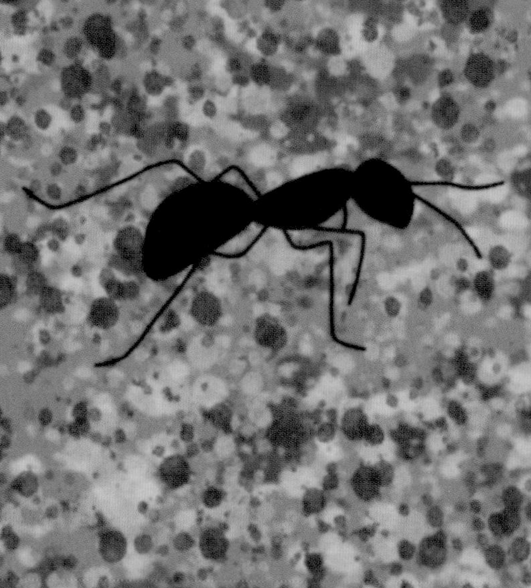

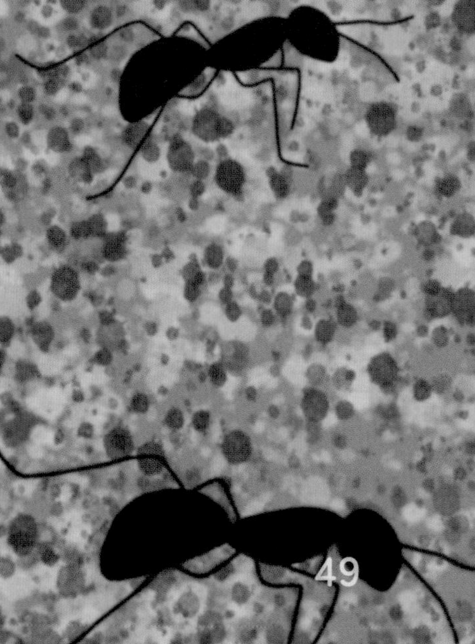

A plan was hatched to rescue Willy Wagtail's egg.

The toads weren't scared of anyone except the bull ants because they could bite and sting the toads and were immune to their venom. Now, Echidna just happened to be best friends with a nearby bull ant colony (but that is another story). She was sure she could get the bull ants to help.

Platypus said he could build a slingshot if Kangaroo was strong enough to fling the ants over to the island to scare away the toads.

Koala said she could climb over the mangrove trees to collect the egg and bring back the ants.

As soon as the ants landed on Toad Island, the toads all jumped in the water and swam away. Koala was watching and waiting nearby in the mangrove trees. As soon as she saw the toads jump in the water, she climbed down onto the island and scooped up the egg. The ants climbed onto Koala's fur and she carried them all back home.

The plan had worked perfectly! That night
Willy Wagtail had her egg safely back in the nest.

When KGB returned to Toad Island, all the toads were groaning as they were covered in lumps from the bull ant bites. They didn't tell KGB they had left the island unguarded.

KGB was relieved when he saw the beautiful, sweet egg still in the nest. As he went to bite the egg, though, it was hard as a rock! He broke his sweet tooth and cried out in pain. Koala had replaced the egg with a stone!

Now the toads and KGB were all moaning so loud that the animals could hear them all across Bush Mob territory.

Gecko was very sorry for stealing the egg. He felt foolish for being tricked by KGB. Thorny Devil and Scrubby Python were also sorry. They just wanted to please Gecko and Bungarra. They all felt shame!

They apologised to Willy Wagtail and told her they would help her anytime she asked. They also brought her fresh insects for breakfast every morning, so she didn't have to leave her nest.

Bungarra was sad he didn't get anything for his birthday. The animals felt sorry for him and decided to make Bungarra a birthday surprise after all.

They collected some honey from the honey ants and river mint from the creek.

Then they rolled a ball of honey in the bright green mint leaves and placed it in a small nest made from dried grass.

The animals presented the honey ball in the nest to Bungarra. The birds sang a beautiful chorus of happy birthday – after all, they had been to choir practice!

Bungarra was so happy. He really did get to eat the sweetest (and brightest) egg of all!

Epilogue

Gecko, Thorny Devil, Scrubby Python, KGB and the cane toads all learnt a very big lesson! They realised it was wrong to steal from others and deceive their friends. It was much better to work together and be kind. That way, everyone can join in on the fun!

About the Author

Helen Milroy

(MB BS, FRANZCP, CATCAP)

These are some of Helen Milroy's first children's books but she is a born storyteller and a talented artist.

Helen is a descendant of the Palyku people of the Pilbara region of Western Australia. She is a child and adolescent psychiatrist and has worked in many different roles during her career. Helen has always been a strong advocate for the mental health and wellbeing of children.

Helen is the WA State Recipient Australian of the Year 2021 and joint winner of the 2020 Australian Mental Health Prize.

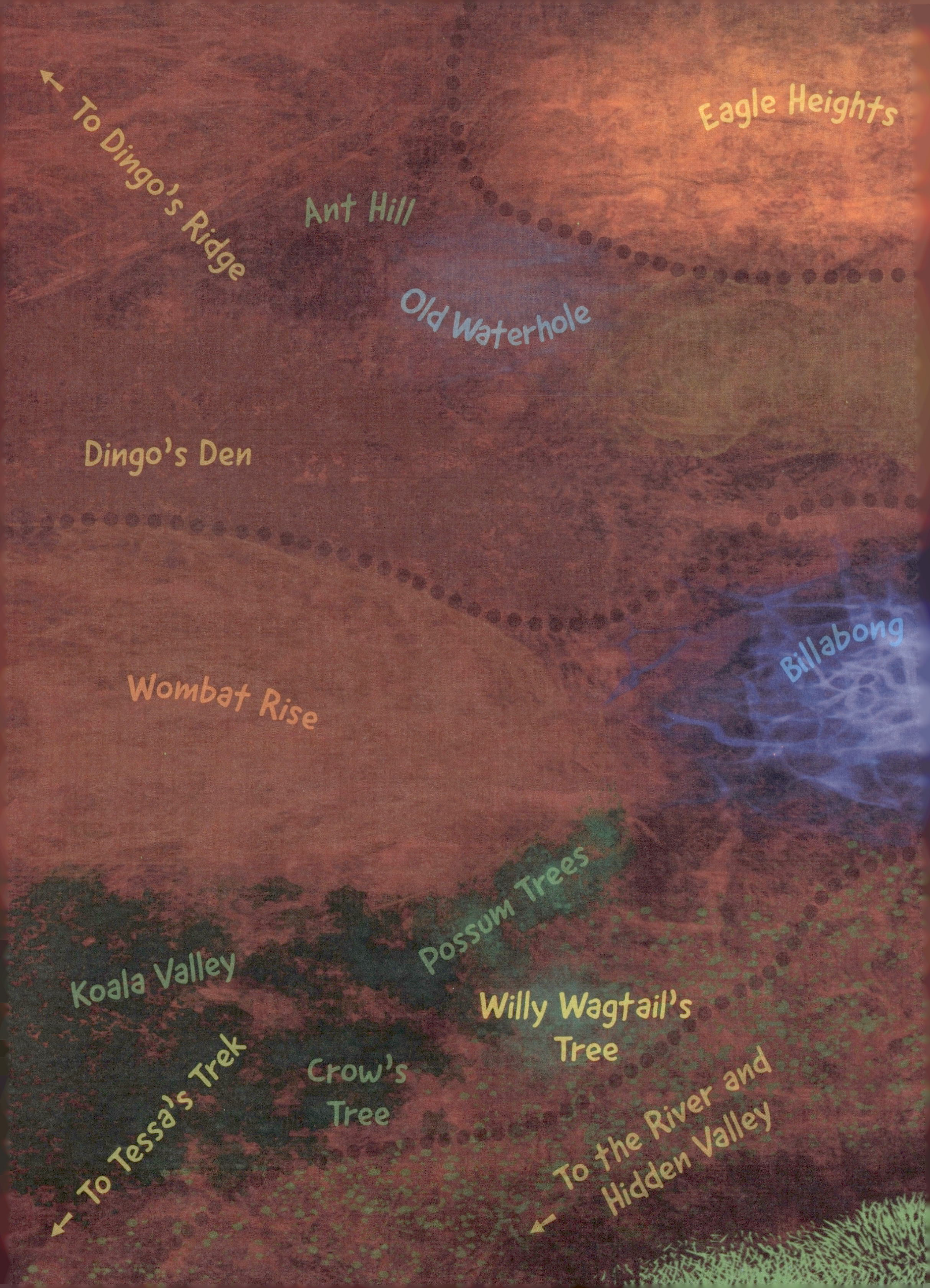

To Dingo's Ridge

Eagle Heights

Ant Hill

Old Waterhole

Dingo's Den

Billabong

Wombat Rise

Possum Trees

Koala Valley

Willy Wagtail's Tree

Crow's Tree

To Tessa's Trek

To the River and Hidden Valley